Angelica looked angrily at the babies. It isn't fair! she thought. Jean-Claude won't play with me. And if he won't play with me, I'm not going to let him play with those dumb babies, either.

She thought for a moment. "The only way to get the DuMondes to leave is to make Daddy come home," she decided.

Angelica came up with a plan.

Rugrats Chapter Books

Bonjour, Babies!

K L a S K Y
C S U P O inc.

Based on the TV series *Rugrats*® created by Arlene Klasky, Gabor Csupo,
and Paul Germain as seen on Nickelodeon®

ISBN 0-439-16502-4

12 11 10 9 8 7 6 5 4 3 2   2 3 4 5/0

Printed in the U.S.A.   40

First Scholastic printing, March 2000

Bonjour, Babies!

by Luke David
illustrated by Jose Maria Cardona

SCHOLASTIC INC.
New York Toronto London Auckland Sydney
Mexico City New Delhi Hong Kong

Chapter 1

It was Saturday morning. Angelica was playing with her Cynthia doll and the Cynthia Dream Four-wheel-drive Vehicle. "D-4-W-D Cynthia . . ." sang Angelica. "She's got it ALL!"

Angelica's mother, Charlotte, was standing nearby. Snapping open her cell phone, she speed-dialed her assistant.

"Jonathan?" said Charlotte. "Cancel my talk today at the Hostile Takeover Huddle. You forgot to put an appointment into my organizer. Yes, yes, you'll have to think of an excuse. I've got to go

to the Lipschitz Never-Too-Early-to-Get-Ready-for-Preschool Fair. Before you know it, our little Angelica will be interviewing!"

Snap! She shut her cell phone.

Angelica's father, Drew, stepped out of the kitchen with a steaming cup of espresso for his wife. Charlotte drank it in one sip before spotting someone through the window.

"Here come Stu and Didi with their boys," she said to Drew. "Are you sure you can handle all the kids by yourself this morning?"

"No problem," said Drew. "Six kids under four—how hard can it be?"

"Vroom!" said Angelica. She drove the D4WD up Drew's leg. It snagged his cashmere pants and pinched his knee.

"SWEETHEART!" yelled her dad. "Please stop!"

Charlotte opened the door, and Tommy toddled in. He ran across the living room to pick up a ball. His mom, Didi, was right behind, carrying baby Dil and three big bags.

"Here, Drew," said Didi. "I've prepared all Dil's bottles for the day and a bag of educational toys and books. Here's his diaper bag, and let me see, I'll set up the Portacrib in your home office."

She lugged Dil and the bags into the next room.

Charlotte waited by the front door for Stu, Tommy's dad.

Woof-woof! barked Tommy's dog, Spike, as he jumped out of the back window of the car. Stu ran after Spike.

"Aw, geez," said Stu, catching Spike by the collar. "Spike must have snuck into the car. Charlotte, can we leave him here too? No pets are allowed at the fair."

"I don't see why not," said Charlotte. "DREW! Here's Spike."

Spike loped into the house and headed straight into the kitchen, where he lay down and quickly fell asleep.

Soon Chuckie arrived with his dad, Chas. "You're a prince to watch the kids today, Drew," said Chas. "And don't worry. With so many of us at the fair, we can cover *all* the bases."

"Yes," added Charlotte, "I'm confident that by the end of the fair we will know which are the top five preschools in town!"

Meanwhile the babies were playing in the living room. Angelica drove the D4WD over Tommy's head. "*Vroom-vroom!*"

"Stop it, Angelica!" yelled Tommy. He walked off with Chuckie.

Dingdong! Dingdong! The doorbell rang again. This time it was Howard and Betty DeVille with their twins, Phil and Lil. The twins ran over to Tommy and Chuckie.

Betty clapped Drew on the back. "Thanks a million for taking care of the pups today," she said. "You're going to have your hands full with *this* crowd. But don't worry, it'll be character-building!"

"Oh, it's not going to be a problem at all," said Drew. "We'll be just fine."

Soon all the grown-ups except Drew piled into the minivan. Drew carried Dil in one arm.

"BURP!" burped Dil, and spat up.

Toot-toot! Charlotte honked the horn as they took off. Drew waggled his elbow before carrying Dil inside and closing the door.

"*Vroom-vroom-vroom!*" Angelica drove the D4WD over Drew's laptop computer on the coffee table.

Deep-deep-neep-neep-nggggggg went the computer, before the screen flashed and then darkened.

Drew gasped. He put Dil down and yelled, "Angelica, honey! Leave my laptop alone!"

Dil began to wail. "Waaaaah! Waaaaaah!"

Drew picked up the baby. "There, there," he comforted Dil.

Beep-beep-beep! went Drew's beeper. He snatched it off his belt and looked at it.

"This code means only one thing—office emergency!" cried Drew. "I've got to get there!"

He plugged a Binky into Dil's mouth. Then Drew looked over at the kids in the playpen.

Lil was pinching Phil's elbow. Chuckie was seeing if his big toe would fit into a baby bottle.

Tommy had taken off his diaper. And Angelica was racing the D4WD through an obstacle course.

"ANGELICA!" yelled Drew again. He put Dil on a cushion and bent down to save the obstacles—which were actually Charlotte's priceless glass figurines.

"DAD-DY! You never let me do anything." Angelica pouted.

Drew looked at his beeper, his watch,

and then at Dil. He scratched his head and rubbed his chin.

Finally, Drew stared upward as he wondered out loud, "But while I'm at the office, who will watch you kids?"

Chapter 2

"Pop—that's who! Pop can baby-sit!" said Drew. "Why didn't I think of that before?" He heaved a sigh of relief as he called Grandpa Lou on the phone.

"Sorry to disappoint you, son," answered Lou. "But I'm going fishing. It's the Lodge's big annual tournament! Can't miss it. Gonna catch *fifteen* big ones today!"

"Thanks anyway, Pop," said Drew. He hung up. Now he heaved a sigh of exasperation. Tommy squirmed away as Drew tried to fasten his diaper.

Chuckie's toe was stuck in the bottle, and he began to whimper. Drew squatted down to help Chuckie. *Plop!* Out popped the toe. Chuckie was relieved.

Suddenly Drew had another idea. "What about Boris and Minka? Maybe they can come over."

Drew dialed Didi's parents, but the phone just kept ringing. Then he remembered. "Drat! It's Saturday—that means they're at the Y playing mah-jongg."

Drew looked out the window. His neighbor Jacqueline DuMonde was working in her garden. He snapped his fingers. "That's it! Jacqui can baby-sit!"

All of a sudden Angelica stopped pouting. She smiled up at Drew. Sweetly she asked, "If Jacqui comes over, can Jean-Claude come too, Daddy?"

Jean-Claude was Jacqui's five-year-old son—and Angelica had a crush on him.

"Sure," answered Drew as he opened

the window and called, "Hello, Jacqui! Can I ask for a big favor?"

Jacqui came over. Drew explained, "I'm in a jam. I'm watching all the kids, but I've got to get to the office. Is there any chance you can pinch-hit for me?"

Angelica jumped up and down. "Ask her! Ask her! PUH-LEEEEZE!"

"Just a minute, Angel," shushed Drew.

"But, of course," answered Jacqui. She was French and spoke with an accent. "I'd be happy to pinch-sit for you." Jacqui giggled at her own joke.

Angelica tugged on her dad's sweater. Drew was about to ask about Jean-Claude when Jacqui asked, "May I bring Jean-Claude with me? He's just inside finishing his breakfast with his papa."

Angelica pumped her fist into the air. "Yessss!" she said.

"Of course," Drew replied as he nodded at Angelica.

"But first, Drew," added Jacqui, "the

babies can help me with the garden, yes? Then I will bring them to your house."

"Sounds good, Jacqui," answered Drew. "We're on our way."

"Wait, Daddy!" screeched Angelica. "I've got to change Cynthia into her gardening outfit."

She tossed the D4WD across the floor. Then she started digging through her Cynthia tote bag to find the gardening outfit.

"Angelica, sweetie," pleaded her dad. "Just bring the whole bag. I've *really* got to go." He steered her out the door with the babies.

In the DuMondes' yard, Drew set Dil down on a blanket beside Jacqui. The other babies started to explore.

There were beautiful flowers and palms all around, and even places with pebbles and sand.

"Bye, kids!" said Drew. "Be good for

Jacqui. And Jacqui, thanks much. I owe you one!" He saluted Jacqui and blew Angelica a kiss.

Angelica barely looked up. She swatted the kiss away. "Whatever," she said. She snapped on Cynthia's gardening knee pads.

"*Bonjour*, babies!" called Jean-Claude. "Hello!"

Angelica perked up. She ran over to her neighbor. "Jean-Claude! Play with me and Cynthia! She has her own sun hat and matching accessories!"

"Look!" Jean-Claude pointed in the other direction. "Phil and Lil are digging up zee worms." He ran past Angelica to the twins.

Angelica flung Cynthia into a flower bed and ran after Jean-Claude.

"Hey, Jean-Claude," said Lil. "You want a worm? They're really yummy!"

"*Oui!*" Jean-Claude said "yes" in French. He had an accent too. "But I do

not think I will eat zee worm. Instead I will see if zee worm will crawl around my finger. Ah, yes, look at that!"

"Yuck!" said Angelica. "I mean, how fascinating!"

Angelica batted her eyelashes at Jean-Claude and smiled brightly, but he didn't notice. Jean Claude watched the worm wriggle up his arm.

Angelica pouted and thought, Jean-Claude isn't being nice to me. She stomped her foot. Well, then, I'll just have to *make* him be nice to me. But how?

Think, think, think. Angelica tapped the side of her head with her finger.

And then she smiled.

Chapter 3

Angelica grabbed a stick from the ground and pretended it was a microphone.

Then she shoved her face in front of Jean-Claude and sang, "I'm a little tugboat, see me pout! Here is my smokestack, here is my snout!"

Jean-Claude looked puzzled. Then he spotted an orange butterfly and ran after it. Angelica skipped behind Jean-Claude.

"Hey, Jean-Claude, I know how to *dance* like a butterfly," she said. "But I'm even prettier than a butterfly. See! Flutter, flutter!" Angelica flapped her arms and did a little leap.

"Very nice," said Jean-Claude. "*Très jolie!*" But he wasn't looking at Angelica. He was looking at the butterfly.

"Hmm," said Angelica to herself. "Singing doesn't work. Dancing doesn't work. I'll try jokes!"

"Hey, Jean-Claude!" she yelled. "What's green and flies?

"Super Pickle!" Angelica laughed, but Jean-Claude didn't.

"What do ducks have for snacks?" she asked, then answered, "Milk and quackers!"

Angelica giggled. But Jean-Claude was busy examining an old bird's nest that had fallen to the ground.

He's forgotten I'm alive, Angelica sighed. Well, now he'll remember!

Angelica snatched the bird's nest from his hand. "That's my bird's nest," she snarled. "What are you doing with it?"

"My apologies, Angelica," said Jean-Claude. "I did not know it was yours. You may have it back, of course."

He handed her the nest and flashed a dazzling smile. Then he headed toward the sandbox where the babies were playing with a dump truck.

Angelica looked angrily at the babies. It isn't fair! she thought. Jean-Claude won't play with me. And if he won't play with me, I'm not going to let him play with those dumb babies, either.

She thought for a moment. "The only way to get the DuMondes to leave is to make Daddy come home," she decided.

Angelica came up with a plan. "I'll pretend that I'm sick. Jacqui will call Daddy. Then she and dumb Jean-Claude will go home!"

Angelica walked over to Jacqui, then grabbed her stomach and doubled over. "Oooh, Jacqui, I have a terrible bellyache!"

"*Cher* Angelica," said Jacqui. "My dear!"

"Call my daddy," said Angelica.

"I have a better idea," said Jacqui. She pulled a green and purple plant from the garden. "Eat this. It is a wonderful cure for zee tummy trouble."

The thought of eating the plant made Angelica really feel sick—and so she was cured.

"That's all right." She sniffed. "Just the smell is good. Yeah, my bellyache is all better now. Thanks, Jacqui."

Angelica walked off in a huff toward the sandbox. On to Plan B, she thought.

Angelica pretended to trip and fall. She grabbed her ankle. "Oooh, Jacqui, come quick!"

"Vhat is it, Angelica?" asked Jacqui.

"My ankle . . . it snapped. I think it's broked. Call my daddy," said Angelica.

Jacqui ran over and knelt beside Angelica. "Let me examine it—"

"Angel-EEEK-a!" called Jean-Claude.

Without thinking, Angelica jumped up on her "bad" ankle. She dashed over to Jean-Claude.

Jacqui shook her head and smiled. Then she got up and went back to her gardening.

At the sandbox Jean-Claude asked, "Angelica? Would you be so kind as to lend us your D4WD? As you can see, we are building a highway."

"Oh! No problem," said Angelica.

Yaaaay! she thought, he wants to play with me after all!

Angelica ran back into her house and brought out the D4WD. "See, Jean-Claude. It has cordoba leatherette seats, the steering wheel turns, and the glove compartment opens—"

"Very nice," said Jean-Claude. "But all we really want is for it to be a hill."

He took the D4WD and planted it in the middle of the sandbox. "We pour this big bucket of sand on top—"

"NOOOOOOOO!" screeched Angelica. "You ruined my D4WD! Jacqui, call my daddy!"

Angelica kicked and threw sand at the other babies. Sand flew all around. It landed in the babies' laps and in their hair. Everybody started to cry.

"HELP!" screamed Chuckie.

"Waaaaaaaaah!" screeched Dil. Jacqui scooped up the baby and put him in the baby swing by the sandbox.

Then, placing her hands firmly on Angelica's shoulders, Jacqui looked steadily into her eyes. "That is enough, young lady," Jacqui said. "Time out!"

Chapter 4

Angelica spent her time-out in a lawn chair by a cactus. She stewed. And while she stewed, she schemed.

"Okay, no more Mr. Rice Guy. Now I go to Plan C. I'll make Jacqui so miserable, she'll want to call my daddy to complain. Daddy will come home and Jacqui will leave, and I'll be rid of her and her stinky little boy forever! But I'm going to need some help. . . ."

Suddenly Jacqui clapped her hands. "*Bien!* Good! Time-out is over, Angelica."

Jacqui had put her gardening tools

away. "Now we will all go to play at *chez* Pickles. Come, children!"

Jacqui carried Dil in her arms as she herded everyone over to Angelica's house.

Inside, Jean-Claude said, "Mama, I will pee-pee in zee toilet now." He went to the bathroom.

Wow, thought Angelica, Jean-Claude is potty-trained, just like me. We really are made for each other! If only he could see it. She sighed. But, alas, it is not meant to be. Then she remembered. Oh, yeah, I forgot. I'm not going to get sad, I'm going to get even.

"Now, Angelica," said Jacqui, carrying Dil on one hip. "Please help watch the babies. I must make one short phone call."

Angelica watched as Jacqui dialed the phone number. "*Bonjour! Oui, c'est moi, Jacqueline. . . .*"

Jacqui was speaking French, which

gave Angelica an idea—a brilliant, awful idea.

"Hey, guys," said Chuckie. "Jacqui's talking funny."

"Don't you babies know anything?" said Angelica. "Jacqui is speaking French. You can't understand . . . but I can, so I'll *transkate* for you. That means I'll tell you what she's saying." She cocked her ear toward Jacqui.

"Ah, *oui*," continued Jacqui, *"bien sûr, nous sommes chez Pickles avec les enfants—Tommy, Dil, Chuckie, Phil et Lil, Angelica. . . ."*

Angelica pretended to gasp. "Oh, no," she said. "Jacqui says that our parents have gone away for a long, long time. And she says she's going to stay with us until they come back"—Angelica paused before adding—"if they ever come back!"

The babies were horrified.

"But who's gonna give me a bath, read to me, and put me to bed at night?" cried Tommy.

"And I gots to see my daddy every day," said Chuckie. "No one else knows how to make my boo-boos better!"

Dil burped and spat up.

"And no one else but Mommy knows how to burp Dil right so he doesn't spit up," added Tommy.

"My mommy gives me noogies," says Phil.

"And my daddy empties the diaper pail," said Lil.

"Waaaaah!" cried the babies all at once. "We want our mommies and daddies!"

Jacqui glanced over at them. She was still on the phone.

"Shhhhh!" shushed Angelica. "Yelling and crying won't work. We've got to make Jacqui *really* miserable. Then she'll call our parents right away and get them to come home so we can see them again."

"Okay, Angelica," said Tommy. "But how?"

36

"Lucky for you I'm really smart and I have a plan," said Angelica. She saw Jean-Claude coming back from the bathroom.

"*Au revoir!*" said Jacqui as she hung up the phone. "Children, I'll be right back. I must take Dil to the kitchen for his bottle."

"Jean-Claude," said Angelica, "I was listening to your mom while you were in the bathroom. Did you know you and she are going to stay here for a long, long time?"

"No," said Jean-Claude. He looked puzzled.

"Yeah," continued Angelica. "Your mom was on the phone. She said that since all of our parents have gone away, you two are going to stay here at my house forever and take care of us."

"How strange!" said Jean-Claude.

"Yeah," said Angelica. "It's more than strange. It means you can say *arf-WAH* to your house, your toys, your dad, and your little dog, Fifi."

"But I do not want to stay here," said Jean-Claude.

Just then Jacqui rushed out of the kitchen.

"Mama?" asked Jean-Claude. "When are we going home?"

Jacqui grabbed Dil's diaper bag. "I have no idea," she answered as she rushed back into the kitchen.

Jean-Claude gasped.

"Don't worry, beret boy," said Angelica. She put her arm around his shoulders. "I'm on the case. . . ."

Chapter 5

Angelica whispered her plan to Jean-Claude. He wanted to see his dad, his dog, and his home. So he agreed to help. All the babies would try to make Jacqui miserable.

Angelica marched to her chalkboard and drew a picture.

"Now," she said. "We've got to do things that Jacqui hates. And there's one thing that grown-ups hate more than anything. Can any of you guess what it is? Here's a clue."

She pointed at her picture of a stick-

figure lady with her fingers in her ears. It looked like she was in pain.

"Earwax?" asked Phil.

"No," said Angelica.

"Fingers in ears?" asked Lil.

"NO!" answered Angelica. "Don't you dumb babies know anything? What grown-ups hate most of all is noise! So let's make as much noise as we can. GO!"

The babies sprang into action.

Phil and Lil ran to switch on the radio and the CD player. Then they switched on the TV. Everything was turned up as loud as it would go.

Chuckie found Angelica's "My Own Karaoke" set and began to sing into the microphone, "LA-LA-LA-LA-LA."

Angelica steered the vacuum cleaner out of the broom closet and began to vacuum. It made a huge sucking sound.

All the noise brought Jacqui out of the kitchen. She held Dil in one arm and the warm bottle in the other.

Tommy ran into the kitchen. He grabbed a bunch of pots and started clanging them together.

Jacqui looked upset for a minute, then realized that even with all the noise the babies were smiling and laughing. So she gave a little laugh and threw her head back. Then she let out a loud, low howl. Dil giggled and began to howl too.

The babies looked at Jacqui. They'd never seen a grown-up howl before.

Tommy stopped clanging his pots. Angelica dropped the vacuum. Chuckie stopped singing. Phil and Lil turned off the TV, the CD player, and the radio.

Everyone laughed and began to howl too. Everyone except Angelica, who folded her arms across her chest. She looked so mad, it seemed as if steam might start pouring out of her ears.

Soon Jacqui stopped howling. "That was very much fun!" Jacqui said. She put Dil in his bouncy seat. "Now I will see what I can find for your snack." She headed back into the kitchen.

Angelica clapped her hands. "Attention, babies," she said. "All right, so our first try was a flop. This next one won't be. I know a little game that's sure to make Jacqui so miserable, she'll want to leave. It's called hide-and-go-peek."

"But Angelica," said Tommy, "growed-ups love to play that with babies."

"Not *this* game . . . *we* don't hide—we hide the baby!"

"But we can't lose Dil," said Chuckie.

"No, Chuckie," said Phil. "We just hide Dil in such a good place that Jacqui can't find him, and she'll *have* to get the growed-ups back to help."

"Ezzakly!" said Angelica.

The babies started looking for the perfect place to hide Dil.

Phil looked in the broom closet. "Very dark, very dusty," he said.

"Wow," said Lil, peering over his

shoulder, "can I hide in there?"

"No," said Phil. "I'm gonna."

"No," said Lil. "I'm gonna. I found it first." They started grabbing at each other.

Angelica pulled the twins apart and said, "Stop squabbling, you two, and get to work. Find a place for Dil and only Dil if you ever want to see your parents again!"

"What about the playpen?" Chuckie asked. "We could hide Dil behind some toys, and it would be nice and safe."

Angelica smirked. "That's a dumb idea. . . ."

"It's not so dumb, Angelica," said Tommy. "It has to be a place Dil likes or he'll start crying, and Jacqui will find him right away."

"All right, Mr. Smarty-pants, where?" asked Angelica.

"Here!" said Tommy. He'd found a big, round table with a cloth that hung all

the way to the ground. "See? Inside it's like a tent. And Dil will like that."

They pushed and pulled Dil in his bouncy seat under the tablecloth. Then the babies put lots of toys around Dil, and Tommy jiggled him until he went to sleep. Then Tommy crawled out.

Just then Jacqui came back into the living room carrying some juice, and apple slices with peanut butter.

Jean-Claude, Angelica, and the babies pounced on the snacks.

"Ah, *bien!*" said Jacqui. "You all were hungry. Now, did Dil finish his bottle? Dil? Dil! Where is Dil?"

Chapter 6

Jacqui looked around. "Oh, have you children hidden zee baby? Hmmm . . . how did you know zee hide-and-seek game is my favorite?

"Ah, where to look first?" Jacqui asked as she headed for the couch. "Did Dil fall behind the cushions? *Non!*"

"He's not anywhere, Jacqui!" said Angelica, hands on her hips. "He's been kittynapped! You'd better get the other grown-ups home right now!"

"I do not think so, Angelica," said Jacqui. She ran into the study. "Is Dil in his Portacrib? *Non!*"

"I'm telling you," screeched Angelica, "Dil is not *anywhere*. Call my daddy!"

"Not yet," answered Jacqui. She ran into the kitchen. "Is Dil in the bread box? *Non!*"

She ran back to the living room. "Is zee baby hiding behind Jean-Claude's blocks? Ah, Jean-Claude, *magnifique!* I see you have built la Tour Eiffel!"

Jacqui ran by the front door. She noticed it had been left open. "Humph," she said. "Dil could not have gone outside, could he?"

"Ah-Ah-Ah-CHOOO!" sneezed Chuckie, who was sitting near Dil's hiding place.

Chuckie's sneeze was so big that he fell onto the edge of the tablecloth and yanked it down.

The knickknacks on the table came clattering off. The tablecloth was pulled up on the other side—and there was Dil.

Jacqui smiled as she knelt down.

"Peekaboo! I see you!" she said.

Dil woke up and began to cry.

"Ah, babeeee-babeeee!" Jacqui knelt down and hugged Dil. "You had a nice little house for zee napping. Now, now, everything is going to be all right. And do you know what? You all gobbled up your snacks so fast that I think you are still hungry. Come, I will get your lunch ready."

Jacqui and Dil headed for the kitchen. Angelica stalled Jean-Claude and the babies.

"Now's our chance," Angelica said.

She put her hands on her hips and narrowed her eyes. "What do grown-ups hate even more than noise, and even more than a lost baby?"

"Carrots and broccoli?" asked Phil. "Or maybe a bottle of sour milk?"

"No . . ." said Angelica.

"Hey, I kind of like sour milk," said Lil.

"Diapie rash?" asked Tommy.

"Think, you dumb babies," said Angelica.

"Camembert cheese that is more cold than zee room temperature?" asked Jean-Claude.

"No, no!" said Angelica.

"Boo-boos?" asked Chuckie.

"NO, NO, NO!" fumed Angelica. "What grown-ups really, really hate is a big mess. So, at lunch, that's just what we'll give Jacqui!"

"Yay!" said Phil.

"Our favorite!" added Lil.

"You got it," answered Angelica. "Food fight!"

The babies trooped into the kitchen. Angelica and Jean-Claude climbed up on their chairs. Jacqui helped the babies into their high chairs. Dil was perched on her hip.

When Jacqui turned to open the fridge door, Angelica gave the command. "NOW!"

Glub! Phil poured yogurt on Lil's head.

Ploppity-plop! Lil tipped the peas down Chuckie's shirt. It tickled. He giggled.

Slosh! Chuckie dumped his apple-sauce onto his high chair.

Skitter-scatter! Tommy tossed two fist-fuls of rice into the air.

Angelica unscrewed the salt shaker and threw salt all around. Jean-Claude sprinkled sugar everywhere too.

Even Dil made a mess. He spat up on Jacqui's shoulder as she turned around.

Taking a deep breath, Jacqui looked at the mess and said, "Ahhhhh . . ."

Then she smiled as Spike got up and gulped down every bit of spilled food from the floor and the furniture.

"Rats!" Angelica muttered to herself. "Foiled again."

Jacqui looked at her.

"I mean, boiled again!" said Angelica. "I love boiled rice!"

"*Bien!*" said Jacqui as she wiped her

shoulder. She looked at the babies. They were all covered with food. "Bathtime!"

Angelica's eyes lit up. She rubbed her hands together with glee. "Perfect!"

Chapter 7

Whoosh! Jacqui ran the water for the bath. Dil was nearby in his bouncy seat.

Jacqui said, "First shift is Tommy, Chuckie, Phil, and Lil. Then after they are clean and dry, they come out, and in go Jean-Claude and Angelica!"

Jacqui undressed the babies and plopped them in.

Whoosh! The water was still running. Angelica smiled up at Jacqui. "Can they have bubbles? Babies love bubbles!"

"But, of course!" answered Jacqui. She handed Angelica the bottle of bubble bath.

"Waaaaaaaaah!" Dil began to howl. Jacqui turned to comfort Dil. "There, there," she said.

Quickly Angelica emptied the whole bottle into the tub. The tub soon filled with bubbles, which started to spill over the side of the tub.

"Wheeeee!" said all the babies.

Jacqui turned around. *"Mon Dieu!"* she cried. "My goodness!" There were bubbles all over the bathroom floor. She reached over the bubbly mountains in the tub and turned off the water.

"This is a disaster, Jacqui," said Angelica. "Call the grown-ups!"

"I do not think that is necessary," Jacqui said. She unplugged the stopper.

As the tub was draining, Jacqui filled her arms with bubbles. She used bubbles to give Tommy a fancy hairdo.

Jacqui made Chuckie a bubble hat. Phil and Lil got bubble beards. The babies laughed. Then Jacqui made her-

self a big bubble bow tie. She tried to make one for Angelica too.

But Angelica wouldn't let her. She stormed out of the bathroom.

"Tsk, tsk!" said Jacqui. "Ah, poor little Angelica!"

Jacqui splashed the babies with water to wash off the bubbles. Then one by one she picked them out of the tub and wrapped them in fuzzy towels.

To Jean-Claude she said, "We will wait for your bath until later. You are not so dirty, anyway."

Jacqui picked up Dil and led them to Angelica's room to get dressed.

Angelica had fallen asleep, angry and exhausted, on her bed. "Shhhhhh!" said Jacqui to the other babies.

Chuckie took one look at Angelica and yawned. Then Tommy yawned. Jean-Claude yawned a really big yawn.

Then Phil and Lil yawned even bigger yawns, and before you knew it, they had all curled up on the soft carpet and were fast asleep.

"How sweet!" said Jacqui. She sat down on the floor beside Dil in his bouncy seat and bounced him gently to sleep.

Soon Jacqui herself yawned the biggest yawn of all and lay down for a nap.

Suddenly someone called, "Hello!" It was Drew. He had come home just as the other grown-ups returned from the Lipschitz Fair. Even Mr. DuMonde had come over with their dog, Fifi.

Woof-woof! barked Spike, leading everyone up the stairs to Angelica's room and waking the babies.

All the babies rushed to their parents. Jacqui handed Dil to Stu.

Drew said, "Jacqui, thank you. Looks like everything's under control here."

"*Ah, oui,*" said Jacqui with a wink to Angelica. "Everything is just fine."

Angelica screwed up her face. Even

though she was finally getting rid of the DuMondes, she felt bad because she had wanted Jean-Claude to like her.

Just then Jean-Claude walked up to Angelica. Taking her hand in his, he said, "Angelica, thank you for a very exciting day. Would you be so kind as to come to my house for a play date tomorrow?" Then he bowed and gently kissed her hand.

Angelica's face lit up. "Okay, Jean-Claude!" she said.

About the Author

Under other pen names, Liza Alexander and June Doolittle, Luke David has written many children's books featuring characters from television. In addition, the author also writes for television, children's magazines, the theater, and the Web.

Like the Rugrats, Luke David's kids, June and Luke, usually do finagle two desserts, and avoid wearing regular pajamas and brushing their teeth when their parents are away. But, unlike the babies in this story, June and Luke always seem to be on their best behavior when their baby-sitter is around. The author lives in Brooklyn, New York.